This is RiSiNg MooN book belongs to:

_____

Do Princesses Scrape Their Knees?

Carmela LaVigna Coyle

illustrated by Mike Gordon
and Carl Gordon

Rising Moon

www.risingmoonbooks.com

Composed in the United States of America
Printed in China

Edited by Theresa Howell
Designed by David Jenney

FIRST IMPRESSION 2006
ISBN-10: 0-87358-909-2
ISBN-13: 978-0-87358-909-3

10   09   08   07   06   5   4   3   2

Library of Congress Cataloging-in-Publication Data

Coyle, Carmela LaVigna.
   Do princesses scrape their knees? / by Carmela LaVigna Coyle ;
illustrated by Mike Gordon.
       p. cm.
   Summary: While a little boy spends a day playing with his older
sister, he asks many questions.
   ISBN-13: 978-0-87358-909-3 (hardcover : alk. paper)
   ISBN-10: 0-87358-909-2 (hardcover : alk. paper)
   [1. Play--Fiction. 2. Brothers and sisters--Fiction. 3. Princesses--
Fiction. 4. Questions and answers--Fiction. 5. Stories in rhyme.]
I. Gordon, Mike, ill. II. Title.

PZ8.3.C8396Dm 2003
[E]--dc22
                                    2006007549

To my husband, Mike:
the athlete, engineer, songwriter, dad, philosopher,
spider-catcher, musician, strongman...

I would also like to acknowledge the sporty girls:
Annie, Maddie, Meg, Kelsey, Phia, Kat, Brooke, Sade,
Milandra, Chloe, and Tahra.
—CLVC

Dedicated to my father
who gave me the greatest gift in life,
my ability to draw.
—M. G.

To my beautiful baby daughter, Melissa.
—C. G.

HEY, SIS, can I play with you today?

I guess that would be okay.

What's it called when you fall head-over-heels?

Princesses call them triple cartwheels.

Will Mom let you skate on the living room floor?

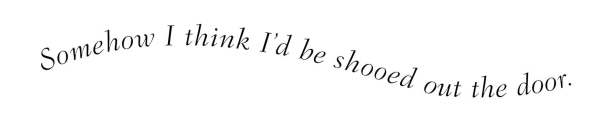

Somehow I think I'd be shooed out the door.

Do princesses put Band-Aids® on their scraped knees?

Princesses can put them wherever they please!

Do you ever get butterflies
inside your belly?

Sometimes my knees feel like
they're made out of jelly.

How do you stay in that yoga position?

Ommmm...I keep my muscles in good condition!

Are you going to kick that ball into the goal?

I'm going to try with my whole heart and soul!

Do princesses ever belly flop?

Sometimes they land with a royal *ker-plop!*

How many times can YOU spin on the ice?

Spinning just ONCE would be oh-so nice.

Are you going to walk
on your toes everywhere?

That would be more than my piggies could bear!

Am I too short to dunk the ball?

With a little help, you're seven feet tall!

Can I ride faster than your speedy pink bike?

It's hard to keep up with my brother's red trike!

Do princesses relax at the end of the day?

That's when they share a chocolate sundae!

When I grow up, can I be sporty like you?

You can do anything you set your mind to.

Win or Lose...

Princesses Rule